DISNEY'S
TREASURE PLANET

nce, long ago, evil pirates sailed through space, stealing treasure from passing ships. The most feared of these pirates was Captain Flint. He hid his stolen treasure, the legendary 'loot of a thousand worlds', in a place so secret, so distant and so mysterious that it had never ever been found.

Years after Flint had disappeared, a boy named Jim Hawkins lived on the planet Montressor with his mother, Sarah. She ran a hotel called the Benbow Inn. Jim's father had left home years before and they were very poor.

ne day a space cruiser crashed near the inn and Jim rushed to see if he could help. The pilot, a turtle-like alien called Billy Bones, was badly hurt. Jim dragged him back to the inn, where he found his mother with her friend, Dr Doppler.

Bones gave Jim a strange sphere. "Beware the cyborg!" he croaked as he took his last breath.

Suddenly, there were pirates everywhere, desperately searching for the sphere. They were furious when they couldn't find it, and set fire to the inn as they fled.

im, his mum and Dr Doppler managed to escape from an upstairs window. They rushed to Dr Doppler's house, where Jim took a closer look at the sphere. It seemed to be like some sort of puzzle. As he fiddled with it, it clicked open and a map appeared. Jim could hardly believe his eyes.

"That's Treasure Planet," he gasped, pointing to a distant green globe. "And it's just a boat ride away. Mum, this is the answer to our problems!"

Sarah was worried about Jim setting off for Treasure Planet, but Dr Doppler reassured her by offering to go too, and keep an eye on the lad. The doctor hired a solar galleon, the *RLS Legacy*, and a crew to sail her.

They met the ship's captain, Amelia. "I don't much care for this crew you hired," she warned Dr Doppler. "They are less than trustworthy." With that she took Jim's map and locked it away safely. Next, she spoke to her first mate. "Mr Arrow, please escort them to the galley straightaway. Young Hawkins will be working for our cook."

he cook was a cyborg called John Silver. A cyborg is a creature that is half alien and half mechanical. Jim gasped as he remembered Billy Bones' words: "Beware the cyborg!" Jim asked the cook if he knew Bones, but Silver shook his head. "Musta been a different cyborg," he assured Jim.

Silver had a cute pet, Morph, who could change shape to look like anyone or anything! When Jim had gone up on deck, Silver frowned. "We'd best keep a sharp eye on this one, Morph. We wouldn't want him straying into things he shouldn't . . ."

ilver soon set Jim to work mopping the deck. As he began, he overheard some of the crew whispering. Suddenly, he was spotted and an ugly creature called Scroop grabbed him. "Cabin boys should mind their own business!" he hissed. Luckily Silver appeared just then and made Scroop let Jim go.

Jim could hardly remember what it was like to have a father, but he felt close to Silver, and trusted him. It was good to have a friend. He worked hard on the ship, but he had a lot of fun and learned many new things along the way.

One night, there was a terrible storm. "Mr Hawkins, make sure all lifelines are secured good and tight!" shouted Captain Amelia above the noise of the storm.

"Lifelines secured, Captain," Jim called back. But then Scroop sneakily cut Mr Arrow's rope and he was lost forever to the endless etherium.

Everyone thought it was Jim's fault.

ext morning, Jim playfully chased Morph into a barrel of fruit and, from inside, overheard Silver and the crew talking. What he heard sent a shiver down his spine. They were planning to mutiny and take over the ship. Jim was devastated. He had trusted Silver.

Suddenly a shout came from up on deck. "Planet ho!" They had reached Treasure Planet.

Jim crept out of the barrel, confused. Was his new friend really a savage pirate? Silver tried to stop him as Jim ran to tell Amelia and Doppler.

"Change in plan, lads!" shouted Silver to the mutinous crew. "We move NOW!"

Amelia, Jim, Morph and Doppler raced to the longboats and took off. The pirates fired laser cannons at them from the *Legacy*, but they managed to crash-land on Treasure Planet. Amelia had been hit and they badly needed somewhere safe to hide.

Jim and Morph had just set off to find somewhere when a strange rickety figure leaped out at them. It was BEN, Flint's old robot! His memory chip was missing, so he wasn't much help, but he gladly let them use his house as a hideout.

But it didn't take long for the pirates to find them. Silver tried everything to get Jim to hand over the map, but Jim just didn't trust him any more.

Silver grabbed the map, but he couldn't open it. Jim saw his opportunity. "You want the map? You're taking me, too," he told Silver stubbornly.

They set off, the map leading them towards a steep cliff. Jim noticed some stange markings on the ground that seemed to match the ones on the sphere. Quickly, he thrust the sphere into a hole right in the centre. Everyone held their breath as Jim pressed a control and, with a brilliant flash, a portal opened. They were able to step right into Treasure Planet's core. "The loot of a thousand worlds," cried Silver, grabbing handfuls of gold.

n the middle of mountains of treasure sat Captain Flint's skeleton, his fist gripping BEN's memory chip. When Jim replaced it, BEN remembered everything, including Flint setting a trap. Soon the planet would explode! "Run, Jimmy!" he shouted.

Jim and Silver leapt onto Flint's old ship as the ground began to shake beneath their feet. Jim fell and Silver had to decide – save Jim or the treasure he had spent a lifetime trying to find? He knew what to do, and together they watched the treasure-filled ship disappear forever before making their way back to the *Legacy*, and home.

Silver knew that Amelia would send him to prison for mutiny, so he stole a longboat and vanished into the etherium. Jim could have stopped him, but knew that if he really cared about Silver, he had to let him go. Silver gave Jim a handful of treasure and left his dear friend Morph to look after him.

Jim used the treasure to rebuild the Benbow Inn and when it was finished, Sarah threw a party for all their friends. The only one missing from the happy reunion was Jim's best friend, a pirate called John Silver.